ESCAPE
from the
DINOSAURS

Caroline Rose
Illustrations by Mike Dorey

BARRON'S

WHOOSH! A burst of flame leapt from the burner. Suddenly, the hot-air balloon lifted right off the ground.

"This is fantastic!" yelled _____. "What a great birthday present!"

As the balloon rose higher, people below shrank into dots, while cars and houses became as small as toys.

"Hey! Be careful not to fall out!" warned the balloonist. The burner made a deafening noise as, grandly, the balloon soared into the sky.

"What makes it go higher?" _____ asked. "Well," said the balloonist, "hot air from the flame fills the balloon. And because hot air expands, it also rises. The balloon acts as a sort of bag, catching the air, and we go up with it as well. We then come down as it cools, so I have to keep putting in more hot air."

"I still think it's magic!" marvelled _____.

THE BALLOON sailed along on a soft breeze. "Why don't we go lower?" suggested _____. "Then we can swoosh upwards like before."

"All right," laughed the balloonist. "It *is* your birthday."

As the balloon lost height, the distant ground grew nearer. But something was odd – the trees were swaying wildly.

"What's happening?" asked _____ nervously.

"Maybe it's the ground that's shaking," joked the balloonist, as he was about to send the balloon shooting upwards with a blast of flame from the burner.

Just then, there came a thunderous roar.

4

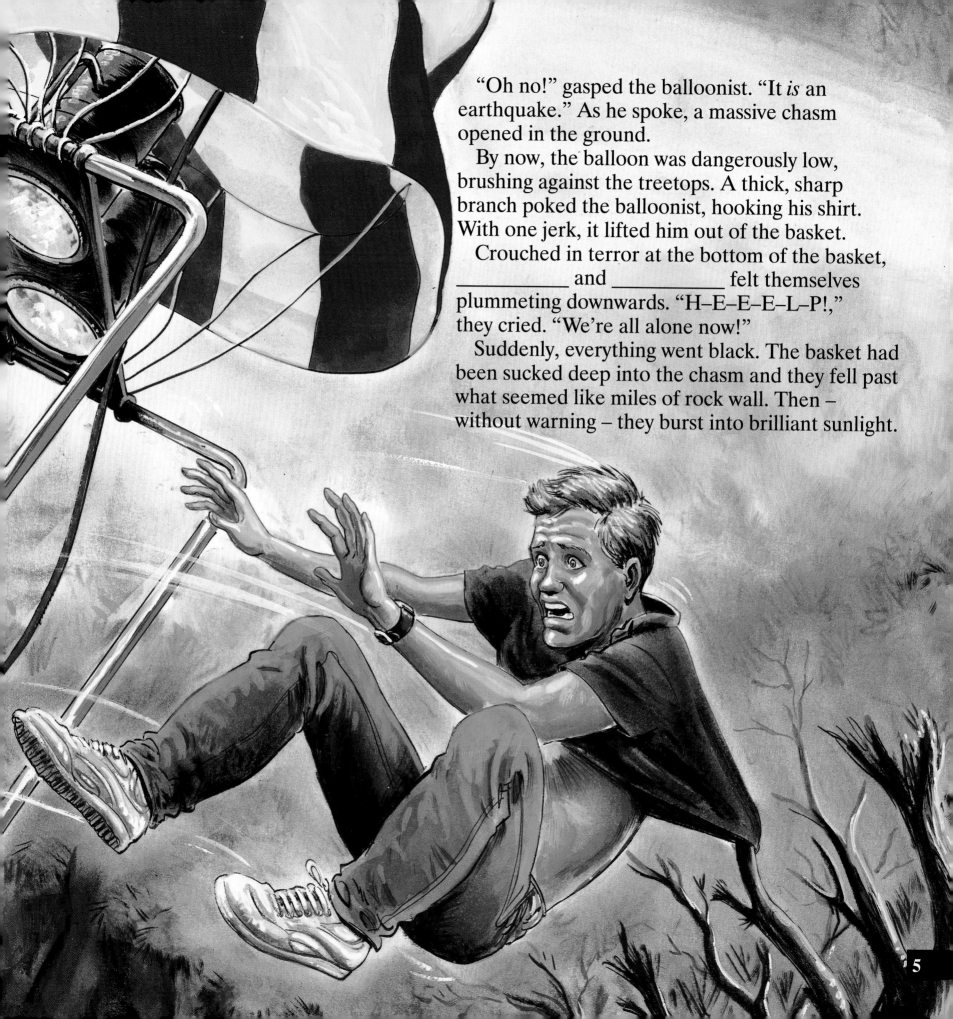

"Oh no!" gasped the balloonist. "It *is* an earthquake." As he spoke, a massive chasm opened in the ground.

By now, the balloon was dangerously low, brushing against the treetops. A thick, sharp branch poked the balloonist, hooking his shirt. With one jerk, it lifted him out of the basket.

Crouched in terror at the bottom of the basket, _____ and _____ felt themselves plummeting downwards. "H–E–E–E–L–P!," they cried. "We're all alone now!"

Suddenly, everything went black. The basket had been sucked deep into the chasm and they fell past what seemed like miles of rock wall. Then – without warning – they burst into brilliant sunlight.

THEY landed, very bumpily, among a clump of huge ferns. Cautiously, they crawled out of the basket.

"Phew!" puffed _____. "Am I glad that's all over! I wonder where we are." They looked around. "It's just like a picture I've seen in a book," said _____.

At that moment, they heard a terrible roar and a giant shadow fell over them. Standing near them was the biggest, and most frightening, creature they had ever seen.

The hungry beast growled at them.
"What *is* it?" gulped _____.
"It's a dinosaur, an **Albertosaurus**," answered
_____.
"It can't be! They're all extinct."
"Not this one!" answered _____. "Anyway,
if I'm right, we're *not* in the twentieth century
anymore."

TIME SEEMED to pass very slowly. Every few minutes, the **Albertosaurus** would peek under the rock, where _____and _____ were hiding.

"Well, if this *is* an **Albertosaurus**, how have we gone back in time?" Neither of them knew.

Suddenly, the **Albertosaurus** dashed away. "Let's see where it went," said _____, plucking up courage.

The two crawled out and saw the monster thundering after another, smaller, dinosaur. _____ recognized it as a **Struthiomimus**. The **Albertosaurus** had decided on a change of menu.

The **Struthiomimus** looked a bit like an ostrich and ran just as fast. But it had arms and no feathers.

"Wow! It can really run!" said _____.

"I wonder if the **Albertosaurus** will catch it!"

At last, the **Struthiomimus** ran between two tall, ferny trees at the entrance to a forest. The **Albertosaurus** was too big to squeeze through. Too late! It had lost its prey. With a bellow of frustration, the **Albertosaurus** lumbered slowly away.

"Well, we can't stay here," said _____. "It's too dangerous. We have to find some way of getting back to our own time."

They were about to set off back to the balloon when loud grunting noises stopped them in their tracks. Their blood froze. "Oh no! What is it *this* time?"

BOTH CHILDREN turned slowly around. There, looking down at them with curious eyes, was a **Maiasaura**. The animal stood on four legs and was the length of a bus.

"It doesn't look fierce," whispered _____, as the animal bent its head to sniff at them.

Both _____ and _____ shut their eyes tightly and made funny faces, thinking its breath was going to be awful. But it was strangely sweet.

"Don't be scared. I don't think **Maiasaura** eat meat," said _____. "I wonder what it wants?"

For a while, _____ and _____ stood rooted to the spot. Then the **Maiasaura** moved slowly away, through the large bushes. Keeping well behind, they followed the **Maiasaura** until it reached an open plain, where there were lots of other creatures just like it. It headed for a circular mound on the ground.

"Look! There are eggs in it. That must be its nest, and *she* must be the mother!" guessed _____ correctly.

"Sssshhh! We'd better get out of here before the others see us," whispered _____ frantically. "They're all guarding their eggs and they might think we're hunters!"

LUCKILY, the balloon did not seem to be damaged too badly. _____ and _____ sat looking at it, wondering what to do.

"Maybe we can make a bonfire," suggested _____, "and fill the balloon with hot air from it. Then we could take lighted branches up with us to keep the air hot." It sounded very dangerous.

"Let's cover it up for now," advised _____. "If we don't, something might come along and use the balloon as a nest!" _____ collected armfuls of the ferny undergrowth, and arranged it over the balloon so that it couldn't be seen.

"Oh, no! It looks like another dinosaur – a **Deinonychus**!" said _____ trembling.

"And what about all that black smoke coming from that mountain over there? What if it's coming from a volcano?"

"If it is, we'd better get out of here. Wait! I'm sure I can hear water. We'll be safer by a river. We can jump in if there's an explosion."

"I hope that **Deinonychus** doesn't follow us," murmured _____.

THE RIVER was flowing quite strongly, past clumps of reeds. Instead of grass, low ferns covered the ground.

Tiny lizards and frogs darted and hopped about in the sun.

One dinosaur, about the size of a chicken, was hunting frogs. Another small creature leapt in the air to catch insects that looked like dragonflies.

"Do you think this water's safe to drink?" asked _____.

"I don't think this place is safe for *anything*. Just look at that!" cried _____ suddenly.

A lot of bones, stained with blood, lay scattered on the ground. A tiny animal, resembling a shrew, was chewing on them.

"What did those bones belong to?" wondered _____.

"Who knows?" replied _____. "Look at those footprints in the mud! Something must have come out of the water and killed it while it was drinking at the river."

"Look behind you!" shrieked _____. "It's... it's the...

DEINONYCHUS!"
It had followed them
after all. "We'd better
not turn our backs!" said
_____.

Still facing the fierce dinosaur, they
edged away. But the **Deinonychus** moved
towards them, and seemed ready to spring.

"Quick, get up that tree!" yelled _____. In
a second, they scrambled up the trunk.

The **Deinonychus** shook the tree with its long arms.
It was not a big dinosaur – only about the size of a
deer – but it had powerful legs. On each foot, it had a
huge, horrible claw that could be flicked forward in
order to slash at its prey.

The palm tree swayed wildly. Then the trunk
snapped. "AAAARRGG–G–H–H–H–H!" screamed
_____ and _____, as they fell, with the
broken tree, into the river.

They clung to the palm as it floated. "Don't let your
feet dangle in the water!" yelled _____.

The palm tree and
its riders were soon whirling about
in the churning flow. The edge of a waterfall
came up all too quickly and over they went.

It was a long drop, but they made it.

"At least we've lost the **Deinonychus**,"
thought _____. The two time-travelers
now crawled out of the water onto the river
bank.

What they did not know was that, nearby,
two big, round eyes were watching closely.

THE **TROODON** was the cleverest of all dinosaurs. A two-legged flesh-eater, it had large eyes for seeing in the dark. This one was mean and hungry. It let out a snarl.

_____ sat up. "What's that noise?"

The **Troodon** stepped out into the open. "Look at that!" gulped _____, pointing at the dinosaur. "Run for it!"

They jumped up and raced along the river edge, the **Troodon** in hot pursuit.

"There!" said _____, pointing to a rocky ledge. "Let's jump onto it, and hide behind the waterfall. Watch out! The ground's very slippery."

But the **Troodon** jumped after them. Then, suddenly, it gave a terrible scream as it slipped and fell backwards.

Blood filled the water as a
beast in the river bit off the **Troodon's** head.
"That was nearly *us*!" gasped _____.
"What if there are others? We'd better get
away from here – fast!"
They stood for a moment, deciding which
way to go. The smoke in the sky, meanwhile,
was getting thicker. The earth rumbled.

"IT *IS* A VOLCANO!" gasped _____.
"We'd better get back to the balloon before we get caught in the lava flow. I'm starving! But I don't fancy eating raw meat – even if we could catch a lizard or something!"

"Isn't that a **Triceratops**?" asked _____. "Maybe we can have some of its fodder. After all, it's a herbivore."

The **Triceratops**, munching on thick leaves, looked at them suspiciously.

"We'll never be able to chew that! It's much too tough," complained _____. Just then, to their delight, _____ discovered a piece of chocolate in a pocket. "Excellent! We can eat at last!" The **Triceratops** looked at the chocolate with interest. "Oh no! You're not getting any of this!" shouted _____.

Smoke from the volcano was now drifting their way, and lots of dinosaurs, sensing danger was afoot, had started to run.

Nearby, a **Parasaurolophus** – a large plant-eating dinosaur – lifted its head. Alarmed by the acrid smell, it boomed a loud sound through the strange hollow tube on top of its head. Then one of its cousins – a **Lambeosaurus** – joined in.

"I have a horrible feeling those are warning signals," said _____ anxiously.

THEY WERE soon surrounded by stampeding dinosaurs. _____ and _____ blundered on, trying to dodge the smaller ones. They had lost track of the river, and now found themselves in a small wood. The sky was getting darker.

"Which way now?" asked _____.

_____ was about to answer when there was a mighty crashing of branches. They turned and, through the dense haze, saw a creature even more terrifying than an **Albertosaurus**.

"**T. REX**!!" screamed _____ and _____. They knew it to be the most fearsome dinosaur that ever lived. Its powerful jaws could have swallowed a human whole.

_____ gripped _____'s arm tightly, hissing: "Run for your life!"

AN AWFUL chase began,
as _____ and _____
dashed through thick bushes and ferns. The
T. rex followed close behind, taking huge steps.
Saliva dripped from its mouth.

"This way! HURRY UP!" yelled _____.
The thunderous footsteps of **T. rex** shook the
ground. Smoke from the volcano stung their
eyes badly.

Then, for an instant, it parted. And there, in
front of them, stood an **Ankylosaurus**.

With the last of their strength, they
clambered onto it. _____ sat on the
creature's neck, gripping its bony horns, while
_____ sat behind, with arms hugging
_____'s waist.

"O-O-UCH!" yelped _____. "A big
spine's sticking right into my rear!"

"Hang on!" shouted _____. "We're
moving!"

They thought they had escaped, but the
T. rex was still on their trail. The giant dinosaur
caught sight of them, and charged.

The **Ankylosaurus** now turned around – away
from the **T. rex** – and, with all its might, swung
its club-like tail. The **T. rex** gave a hideous
scream as its leg-bone broke under the impact.
_____ and _____ stared in
amazement. The **Ankylosaurus** had defeated
the biggest bully on earth!

AS THE **ANKYLOSAURUS** lurched forward, _____ and _____ gripped its spines.

Suddenly, the ground shook violently, and they were almost thrown from the beast. With a mighty blast, the volcano erupted, sending out steam.

Terror spread among all the dinosaurs. From their high perch, _____ and _____ watched hundreds of creatures fleeing the noise and heat.

"We must be back near the balloon!" yelled _____. "Look! Here are all the **Maiasaura** nests."

The **Maiasaura** mothers were desperately trying to protect their youngsters from sharp-toothed predators.

The two bareback riders scrambled off the **Ankylosaurus**. "Let's hope the balloon's still there!"

"What's that red, gloopy stuff rolling towards us?" asked _____.

"That's boiling hot lava, from inside the volcano! It's coming our way fast! RUN!!"

LUNGS BURSTING, _____ and _____ reached the balloon. They had started to remove the ferns covering it, when _____ yelled: "HEY! Some **Maiasaura** babies have gotten into the basket!"

How were they going to get off the ground? Just then, there was a terrific rush of hot wind. What luck!

_____ and _____ jumped in the basket and held the mouth of the balloon wide open.

As the balloon filled, it lifted, and soon the basket, too, began to rise. They were only a few feet above the ground when a mother **Maiasaura** came bounding up. She leapt at the basket, attacking it with her forelegs.

"What does she want?" screamed _____. They clung to the sides of the basket, terrified that it would crash at any minute. If it did, they might have to stay in the prehistoric world forever! Their bones would be dug up millions of years later.

What a surprise for the paleontologists of the future!

Torrents of lava and flames belched out. The heat blew down the valley and swept the balloon high into the air.

U P AND UP, the balloon shot. _____ and _____ looked at each other in alarm.

Something rustled. Then a tiny head popped up. It was a baby **Maiasaura**! Another one joined it.

"No wonder the mother was so upset. She thought we'd kidnapped her children!"

The balloon was now floating through white, billowing clouds. Suddenly, all was plunged into darkness. It seemed an age before they could see again. At once, they recognized the twentieth-century landscape from which the balloon had first taken off. Sunlight flickered through the roots of trees. The balloon now came level with the grass. _____ and _____ tipped out.

The **Maiasaura** babies scampered off into the woods. They did not try to stop them. What now caught their attention was the siren of a vehicle that was coming to the rescue. What a story _____ and _____ could tell!

"But who on earth's going to believe us?"

DINOSAUR DATA

All the dinosaurs featured in your adventure lived in what is now western North America in Cretaceous times – that's between 135 and 65 million years ago. Here is some more information about them.

ALBERTOSAURUS (al-BERT-oh-SAW-rus) was a smaller relative of the fearsome Tyrannosaurus rex but, at 29 feet (9 meters) long, it would have still towered over you! This huge carnivore (meat-eating) dinosaur gets its name from the place where its remains were discovered – Alberta, in Canada.

ANKYLOSAURUS (an-KY-low-SAW-rus) was over 32.81 feet (10 meters) long and built like a tank. It was covered in bony plates and had a deadly club on the end of its tail. But it was a herbivore, or plant-eater, and would only have attacked if threatened.

DEINONYCHUS (DIE-no-NIKE-us) was only man-sized but it made a terrifying enemy for many a larger dinosaur. Deinonychus' name means 'terrible claw' and it is called this because of the sharp curved, claws on its feet. It was probably a fast runner and chased its prey across prehistoric Montana.

MAIASAURA (MY-a-SAW-ra) was a family-loving dinosaur, whose name means "good mother lizard." It was about 29 feet (9 meters) long, ate plants and lived peacefully in groups or herds.

PARASAUROLOPHUS (par-a-SAUR-oh-LOAF-us) was a strange-looking dinosaur, famous for the large hollow crest on it head. Scientists believe that this huge herbivore could have made deep sounds by blowing through the crest.

STRUTHIOMIMUS (STROOTH-ee-oh-MIME-us) looked so much like an ostrich that scientists called it by a name meaning "ostrich mimic." It was about as tall as a man and had long legs to escape from predators.

TRICERATOPS (try-SER-a-tops) had three deadly horns on top of its head which would have made other dinosaurs think twice before attacking it. Triceratops looked fierce but was actually a plant-eating dinosaur. This bulky beast weighed up to 12 tons, or 24,000 pounds!

TROODON (TROE-o-don) is thought to have been one of the cleverest dinosaurs, with a large brain for its size. It was also one of the smallest dinosaurs, but this little meat-eater had sharp claws and was far from helpless.

TYRANNOSAURUS REX (tie-RAN-oh-SAW-rus RECKS), the most famous of all the dinosaurs, was probably also the fiercest. This was a massive carnivore – 46 feet (14 meters) long and 20 feet (6 meters) tall. It had gigantic jaws and lots of sharp teeth, like steak knives, with which it ate its victims. Its name means "king of the tyrant reptiles." Look out for T. rex in your adventure!

Copyright © 1994 Quartz Editorial Services, 112 Station Road, Edgware, England HA8 7AQ

U.S. edition copyright © 1995 Barron's Educational Series, Inc.

All inquiries should be addressed to:
Barron's Educational Series, Inc.
250 Wireless Boulevard
Hauppauge, NY 11788-3917

ISBN 0-8120-6557-3

PRINTED IN HONG KONG
5678   9927   987654321